TAKE A RIDE
BY MY SIDE

TAKE A RIDE
BY MY SIDE

Written by JONATHAN YING
Illustrations by VICTORIA YING

HARPER
An Imprint of HarperCollinsPublishers

Take a Ride by My Side
Text copyright © 2018 by Jonathan Ying
Illustrations copyright © 2018 by Victoria Ying
All rights reserved. Manufactured in China.

www.harpercollinschildrens.com

ISBN 978-0-06-238070-8 (trade bdg.)

The artist used Adobe Photoshop to create the digital illustrations for this book.
Typography by Jeanne L. Hogle
18 19 20 21 22 SCP 10 9 8 7 6 5 4 3 2 1

First Edition

This one's for Kirsten—we would never have
gotten this far without you
—J.Y.

To my Travel Buddy, Bonnie Lu
—V.Y.

The sun is shining—what a day!
Grab your bags. Let's go away!

We'll take a trip!

A trip to where?

Let's take a trip from here to there.

Let's start our trip out with a hike.

But I'd prefer to ride a bike.

A great idea! I'll join your ride,
and we can travel side by side.

Are we here? That sure was fun!

Not yet. We've only just begun.

Oh no—we're stuck! The bridge is gone.

No need to worry—just hang on.
I've got a plan. Here's what we'll do:
We'll get there in a long canoe.

Across the sea we'll stay afloat.
We'll get some help from that tugboat!

Toot toot! This tugboat's really strong.

Thanks for taking us along!

From here, let's drive a submarine
to the prettiest place we've ever seen.

We'll pass a ray, a friendly shark . . .

and a fish that glows bright in the dark.

Is this the place we're meant to be?

Oh no, there's still much more to see.

Up, up, up! It's time to fly
a great big airplane through the sky.

What a view! We must be here!

No, not quite yet. But have no fear.
Our rocket ship is launching soon.
It's time to see the big, bright moon!

Wow, that rocket sure was fast.
We've made it to the moon at last!

And guess where else we are,
just look—

the final pages of our book.

What a trip! That sure was grand.
We sailed the sea and crossed the land.

But even though it's fun to roam,

there's nowhere quite as great as home.